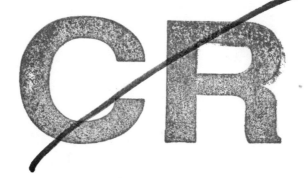

BEAUTY and the BEAST

With illustrations selected and arranged
by Cooper Edens
from the Green Tiger's collection of old children's books

The Green Tiger Press Inc. • San Diego

This version copyright © 1989 by Cooper Edens
Library of Congress Catalog Card No. 88-081988
Hardbound ISBN 0-88138-115-2
3 5 7 9 10 8 6 4
Manufactured in Hong Kong

The Story

The idea of a woman marrying an animal which later is revealed as a human being is widespread in world folklore. The ancient story of Cupid and Psyche is similar in many details, though tragic in its conclusion. The 17th century *Pentamerone* includes two tales which closely parallel *Beauty and the Beast*. In 1740 Madame de Villeneuve published a collection of stories which included a very long version of the beauty and the beast story. In 1756 Madame Marien Leprince de Beaumont published a collection of tales, *Magasin des enfans*, in which the story is given a final purification into the form we know today. The next year this was translated into English, and since then has appeared in myriad retellings.

For this edition we have combined several late 19th century retellings for children. This treatment is less literary, more basic and pungent, and seems to us the perfect foundation for a pictorial version.

The Illustrations

I have undertaken to illustrate this book with pictures from many illustrated versions. This is obviously an instructive way to approach the subject. One can learn by comparison how different artists see the same characters and scenes. By simply leafing through this volume one learns a great deal about the viewpoint and style of the illustrators involved. Further, one is forced to confront the fact that there is no inevitable path to the vivification of a text, that the artist is confronted with almost an infinitude of choices. Surprisingly, it is also an exciting and effective way to tell a story. No one artist sees every episode with equal clarity. By this method the best version of each moment can be used. Furthermore, the universal power of the myth is superbly emphasized by the different visions. Any artist's view of Beauty seems too specific. If one writes that she is young and blonde and blue eyed, the reader finds

himself, after a time, doubting that this is indeed the perfect embodiment of the idea. But if she is constantly mutating—now blonde, now brunette; now fragile, now stately; now 18, now 30; now tall, now short—then one believes. For the Beast it is the same problem, and the same rightness in change. He is, in this version, lion, wolf, rodent, bear, boar, elephant, walrus, minotaur, and other forms combining these and other elements. How much more mysterious and believable is this form-shifting beast.

I hope you will enjoy reading, and studying, this version of a lovely tale.

Cooper Edens

4

BEAUTY and the BEAST

ONCE
there was a
rich merchant
who had a noble
house of his own, and
many goodly ships upon the seas. He had
three daughters, all handsome; but the best in
outward and inward charms was the young-
est, who, from childhood, went by the name
of Beauty. She was the pet of everybody but
her two vain, giddy sisters. Beauty loved to go
about doing good: she visited the homes of
the poor and aided them in their troubles,—
which was gall to her idle, teasing sisters.

A wicked lawyer, by his artful conduct in
a lawsuit, brought Beauty's father to the brink
of poverty; and, to crown all, word came that
all his richly-laden ships were lost at sea, making him a ruined man. He had only enough
left to rent a small cottage in the country,
where he had to live in a very humble way,
and that by labour.

Beauty and fidelity were one. She loved her father the more because of his misfortunes, and she would not be parted from him, although the work she had to do was made irksome by the spiteful words of her sisters.

When they had lived in the cottage a year, the merchant received a letter which made his eyes sparkle with delight. It told him to hasten to the next seaport town, for the largest of his ships, which was said to have been lost, had arrived in harbour, and the captain wished to hand over the goods to him. The elder sisters danced for joy, for they believed they would leave the dull place and have all things fine again; they urged their father to set off at once, and made him promise to buy them rich dresses and all kinds of jewellery.

"Beauty," said her father, "have you no favour to ask at my leave-taking? What shall I bring you when I return?"

"Well, father," she said, "to satisfy me that you have been thinking of me, bring me a red rose, for we have no roses in our garden."

The daughters, going with their father to the door, waved their napkins as he rode off.

When the merchant reached the seaport and the harbour, he found, to his utter dismay, that he had been cruelly cheated—no ship was there, and he turned homeward weary and sad of heart. When he was within fifty miles of home it began to rain heavily, with a strong wind; and darkness coming on, he lost his way. All at once he saw a yellow light in the distance, and on reaching it, he found himself in front of a grand palace. Entering the court-yard and looking about, he saw a stable with the door open, into which his horse walked, and where he helped himself to a plentiful supply of fodder. The hall door of the mansion also stood open, into which the merchant entered, and he was amazed at the awful stillness around. He passed through several rooms, and then entered one with a large fire on the hearthstone, and a sideboard laden with all kinds of food. On a small table was a silver plate with one knife and fork.

He hung his wet riding-cloak over a
screen, then sat down and ate a hearty meal.

He next came to a small room where there was a bed with the sheets turned down.

"Oh, I see it all now!" he said, speaking to himself. "This is the home of a good fairy, who takes care of poor travellers like myself." He undressed, climbed into the bed, and was soon fast asleep.

When he awoke and got up, he looked out of the window and saw bowers covered with lovely flowers of every form and hue. On his way to the stable to look after his steed, he passed under an archway covered with red roses, and plucked one to carry home to Beauty.

All at once he heard a frightful growl, and saw a wild-looking monster coming towards him, so that he could not stir for fear.

"Thankless wretch!" roared the Beast, with a hoarse voice, "I saved your life by finding you food and shelter; in return you steal my roses. But your life shall pay the cost; in a quarter of an hour you shall die."

"Pardon, my lord," said the merchant. "I am now very sorry that I took the rose; it is to give to one of my daughters, who is fond of roses."

"Hold there!" roared the angry creature. "I am no lord; I am a beast, and hate the crafty flattery of men. How many daughters have you?"

"Three, my lor—I mean beast," said the merchant.

"Well, then," said the monster, "I will let you go home if one of them will agree to die in your place. So away. If they cannot agree, you shall return to me in three weeks."

The fond father would rather have died then, than that any one of his daughters should lose her life. He was glad of one thing, however: by obeying the Beast, he would be able to see them again before he died.

16

He therefore started for home, which he
reached in a few hours. When his daughters
met him they were downcast at his sadness.

Presenting Beauty with the fatal rose.
"Take the flower," he said; "It has been pur-
chased with the life of the one you love best."

He then told his daughters all that had happened at the palace of the Beast.

The three weeks soon passed away, and Beauty prepared to go along with her father. He tried to prevent her, but she insisted. "Father," said Beauty, "though I am young I am not afraid to die; I would rather be killed by the monster than die broken-hearted knowing that he had killed you."

The morning came when the journey must be taken. The elder sisters made a show of grief. The father was filled with real sorrow, and found his only comfort in Beauty, who cheered him on the way.

When they arrived at the palace the doors opened of themselves; sweet music was heard, and they walked into a large hall, where, being weary, they sat down. But they did not sit long, for a loud growl was heard near. Starting up, the father clung to his child to protect her, as the Beast strode into the hall.

"Did you make this journey of your own free will?" asked the Beast of Beauty.

Beauty, trembling, stammered out, "Y-e-s."

"You answer well," said the Beast. "You are a good lady, and I thank you." Turning to the merchant, he said, "Good sir, you may rest here for the night, but on the morrow you shall leave here and never return.—Good-night, Beauty."

"Good-night, Beast," she said; and the monster retired.

21

It was comforting to the father to notice
the changed tone and manner of the Beast in
the presence of his child, and more so when,
next morning, Beauty related to him what she
took to be a dream, in which a fairy-like dam-
sel stood by her side and said to her, "Fear
not; I will keep you from harm: the love you
have shown to your father who is in sorrow,
must not go without reward."

The time came for the father to go away.
The Beast loaded his horse with as much gold
as he could carry. Despite this, the father was
deeply grieved at the parting. Beauty tried to
cheer him by saying that she would try to
soften the heart of the Beast, and get him to
let her return home soon. After he was gone,
she went into a fine room, on the door of
which was written, in letters of gold, "Beauty's Room;" and lying on the table was a por-
trait of herself, under which were these
words: "Beauty is Queen here; all things will
obey her."

One night at supper, the Beast told
Beauty that she alone commanded there. "I
do not," said he, "pretend to have any will. I
am under your orders: if you dislike my presence I will go away; but tell me, do you not
think me very ugly?"

"To tell the truth," said she, "I do; but
then I am certain you are very good."

"My nature," said he, "is a good one, but
everybody knows I am a monstrous creature."

25

"For all that," said she, "I would rather have goodness under an ugly form than evil hidden under a form of beauty. I remember having seen many brutes in the form of men."

Often the Beast would say on his knees before this adored one, "Beauty, be my wife." To such words Beauty would never listen.

He would then bid her "Good-night" with a sad voice, and she would retire to her bed-chamber.

The palace was full of galleries and apartments, containing the most beautiful works of art. In one room was a cage filled with rare birds. Not far from this room she saw a numerous troop of monkeys of all sizes. They advanced to meet her, making her low bows. Beauty was much pleased with them and said she would like some of them to follow her and keep her company. Instantly two tall young apes, in court dresses, advanced, and placed themselves with great gravity beside her, and two sprightly little monkeys took up her train as pages. From this time the monkeys always waited upon her with all the attention and respect that officers of a royal household are accustomed to pay to queens.

Beauty was now, in fact, quite the Queen of the palace, and all her wishes were gratified; but, excepting at supper-time, she was always alone; the Beast then appeared, and behaved so agreeably that she liked him more and more. But to his question, ''Beauty, will you marry me?'' he never could get any other answer than a shake of the head from her, on which he always took his leave very sadly.

Although Beauty had everything she could wish for she was not happy, as she could not forget her father, and brothers, and sisters. At last, one evening, she begged so hard of the Beast to let her go home that he agreed to her wish, on her promising not to stay away longer than two months, and gave her a ring, telling her to place it on her dressing-table whenever she desired to go or to return; and then showed her where to find suitable clothes, as well as presents to take home.

The poor Beast was more sad than ever. She tried to cheer him, saying, "Beauty will soon return," but nothing seemed to comfort him. Beauty then went to her room, and before retiring to rest she took care to place the ring on the dressing-table. When she awoke next morning, great was her joy at finding herself in her father's house, with the gifts and clothes from the palace at her bed-side.

At first she wondered where she was; but she soon heard the voice of her father, and, rushing out, she flung her arms round his neck. The father and daughter had much to say to each other. Beauty related all that had happened to her at the palace. Her father, enriched by the liberality of the Beast, had left his old house, and now lived in a very large city, and her sisters were engaged to be married to young men of good family.

When she had passed some weeks with her family, Beauty found that her sisters, who were secretly vexed at her good fortune, still looked upon her as a rival, and treated her with coldness. Besides this, she remembered her promise to the Beast, and resolved to return to him. But her father and brothers begged her to stay a day or two longer, and she could not resist their entreaties. But one night she dreamed that the poor Beast was lying dead in the palace garden; she awoke in a fright, looked for her ring, and placed it on the table. In the morning she was at the Palace again, but the Beast was nowhere to be found: at last she ran to the place in the garden that she had dreamed about, and there, sure enough, the poor Beast was, lying senseless on his back.

At this sight Beauty wept and re-
proached herself for having caused his death.
She rose from his side, and bringing water in
a pearl shell, bathed his face. The Beast
opened his eyes, looked up to her, and feebly
said, "Beauty, you have forgotten your promise; but I die happily, since you are the last
form my dying eyes can look upon."

"Dear Beast," said Beauty, "you must not die: live to be my husband. Here, behold me kneeling at your side. I will be your wife—truly your own."

The moment Beauty had spoken, the front of the palace glowed with lights. Lamps of all colours appeared among the trees. Fireworks streamed into the air, and sweet music sounded everywhere. The whole space was peopled with pages and servants. Beauty took no notice of all these.

Her surprise was great when, instead of the ugly form she was accustomed to see, a handsome prince knelt before her, kissed her hand, and thanked her for having broken the spell.

"But where is the Beast?" cried Beauty.

"Behold him at your feet, fair Beauty," he said; "for I am he. A wicked fairy had condemned me to remain under the shape of a beast till a beautiful virgin should consent to marry me. You judged of me by the goodness of my heart; in return I offer you my hand."

Beauty helped the prince to rise, and arm in arm they walked toward the palace.

There she rejoiced at finding her father and sisters waiting, for they had been conducted to the place by the good fairy she had once beheld.

"Beauty," said this good fairy, "come and receive the reward of your choice. You are going to be a great queen; I hope the throne will not lessen your virtue.—As for you, ladies," said the fairy to Beauty's two sisters, "I know your hearts, and all the spite they contain. Become two statues, but still retain your reason. You shall stand before your sister's palace-gate, and be it your punishment to behold her happiness."

The prince married Beauty, and their happiness was complete, because it was founded on goodness.

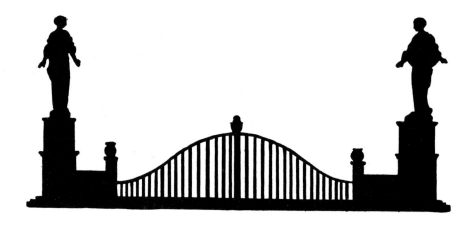

Acknowledgements

front cover	Anonymous German illustrator
frontispiece	E.V.B., *Beauty and the Beast*, nd
copyright page	Gordon Browne, *The Queen of Hearts and Other Plays*, 1919
page 3	Anonymous, *The Ideal Fairy Tales*, 1897
4	Margaret Evans Price, *Once Upon a Time*, 1921
6	Edmund Dulac, *The Sleeping Beauty and Other Fairy Tales*, 1910
7	Anonymous, *The Ideal Fairy Tales*, 1897
9	Anonymous, *The Favourite Book of Nursery Tales*, 1893
10	E.V.B., *Beauty and the Beast*, nd
11	E.V.B., *Beauty and the Beast*, nd
12	Edmund Dulac, *The Sleeping Beauty and Other Fairy Tales*, 1910
13	M.B., *Old Fairy Tales*, nd
14	Walter Crane, *Goody Two Shoes' Picture Book*, nd
15	Lancelot Speed, *Fairy Tale Plays*, 1913
16	W. Heath Robinson, *Old-Time Stories*, 1921
17	Anonymous, *The Favourite Book of Nursery Tales*, 1893
18	Walter Crane, *Goody Two Shoes' Picture Book*, nd
19	Margaret Evans Price, *Once Upon a Time*, 1921
20	Anonymous, *The Favourite Book of Nursery Tales*, 1893
21	Charles Robinson, *The Big Book of Fairy Tales*, nd
23	Anonymous, *The Ideal Fairy Tales*, 1897
24	E.V.B., *Beauty and the Beast*, nd
25	Walter Crane, *Goody Two Shoes' Picture Book*, nd
26	Anonymous, *Old Fairy Tales*, nd
27	Anonymous, *My Nursery Tale Book*, nd
28	Margaret Evans Price, *Once Upon a Time*, 1921
29	Walter Crane, *Goody Two Shoes' Picture Book*, nd
30	Charles Robinson, *The Big Book of Fairy Tales*, nd
31	Margaret Evans Price, *The Big Book of Fairy Tales*, 1921
33	Arthur Rackham, 1915
34	H.J. Ford, *The Blue Fairy Book*, 1889
35	Anonymous, *The Favourite Book of Nursery Tales*, 1893
36	Walter Crane, *Goody Two Shoes' Picture Book*, nd
37	Edmund Dulac, *The Sleeping Beauty and Other Fairy Tales*, 1910
38	Anonymous, *The Ideal Fairy Tales*, 1897
39	Anonymous, *The Favourite Book of Nursery Tales*, 1893
40	Charles Robinson, *The Big Book of Fairy Tales*, nd
41	E.V.B., *Beauty and the Beast*, nd
42	Margaret Evans Price, *Once Upon a Time*, 1921
43	Anonymous, *The Ideal Fairy Tales*, 1897
44	Gordon Browne, *The Queen of Hearts and Other Plays*, 1919
colophon	Gordon Browne, *The Queen of Hearts and Other Plays*, 1919
back cover	Warwick Goble, *The Fairy Book*, 1913

The typeface is Windsor Light, set by
Professional Typography, Inc. of San Diego, California.
Color separations, printing and binding by
Colorcraft of Hong Kong.